Elder Park Library
228a Langlands Road
Glasgow,
G51 3TZ
Phone/Fax: 0141 276 1540/1

This book is due for return on or before the last date shown below. It may
be renewed by telephone, personal application, fax or post, quoting this
date, author, title and the book number

Glasgow Life and its service brands, including Glasgow
Libraries, (found at www.glasgowlife.org.uk) are operating
names for Culture and Sport Glasgow

First published in Great Britain in 2015
by Hodder Children's Books
The rights of Vivian French and David Melling to be identified as the Author and
Illustrator of the Work have been asserted by them in accordance with the Copyright,
Designs and Patents Act 1988.

3 5 7 9 10 8 6 4

A Catalogue record for this book is available
from the British Library

ISBN 978 1 444 92228 8

Printed and bound in Great Britain by
Clays Ltd, St Ives plc

The paper and board used in this book are made from wood from responsible sources.

Hodder Children's Books
An imprint of Hachette Children's Group
Part of Hodder and Stoughton
Carmelite House
50 Victoria Embankment
London EC4Y 0DZ

www.vivianfrench.co.uk   www.davidmelling.co.uk

For the wonderful children and staff at Oasis
Academy Short Heath, Birmingham, with love.
VF

In memory of Zorka Maričić
DM

Dora

Sam J. Butterbiggins
and Dandy the doodlebird

Hazel

Prunella

Horace

Uncle Archibald

Aunt Eglantine

A DISASTROUS MORNING

Dear diary,

My ambition is to be a Very Noble Knight who rides a snow-white steed (that's the kind of horse Very Noble Knights ride) and who does Noble Deeds and goes on quests.

It was nearly time for lunch, and Sam J.
Butterbiggins was sitting up in his tower
bedroom trying to write his diary. There was
a smear of ink on his nose, and his fingers were
an interesting shade of blue – Sam was not a
tidy writer. He sucked the end of his pen, and
looked out of the window.

Outside, the sky was blue and the sun was shining, and the forest that surrounded Mothscale Castle on three sides was looking green and cheerful. Usually it was dark and gloomy, and Sam suspected that unpleasant things lurked in the shadows beneath the trees. Cheered on by the sunshine, he turned back to his ink-spattered page.

I don't care what
Aunt Egg says.
I'm sure there
are wolves in the
woods. I can hear
them howling at night.
I think the trees move,
too. I'm CERTAIN one
waved to me when I was

*looking out of the window yesterday evening.
I waved back, just to see what happened,
and it waved again from a different place!*

*I wonder if Mother and Father know how
weird Mothscale Castle is?*

Sam glanced up at the portrait of his parents
that hung above his bed. They leered happily
into a corner, and Sam shook his head at them.
"It's all very well for you, going away for a
whole year. But what about me? Stuck here
with Aunt Egg and Uncle Archibald, and only
Prune for company—"

"AWK!" The doodlebird gave Sam a
reproachful look from his perch on top of
the door.

Sam grinned at him. "Sorry, Dandy. And
you, of course. And ..." he patted an old and
grubby parchment scroll lying on the table

beside him, "I've got this now!"

The doodlebird nodded several times and flew down to Sam's shoulder. "AWK," he said, and nibbled his ear.

"It's all right," Sam said. "I was just about to write about it." He dipped his pen in the inkwell, and began again.

Guess what - the most AMAZING thing happened! I found an ancient scroll, and it said,

"Greetings to all who wish to be Truly Noble Knights. Herewith we offer you the tasks that should be accomplished, in order as hereby listed, that ye may succeed."

If I can do all the tasks, then maybe I'll get to be a real knight! But I've only just started.

Task one: Thou shalt find thyself a true companion.

I've actually done that one. My true companion is Prune, my cousin. She's a bit annoying, but not all the time. Also she has a pony called Weebles, so when I get my snow-white steed we'll be able to go on quests together. At first she wanted to be a knight and I got REALLY worried

because I thought I'd have to be the True Companion, but then she changed her mind. PHEW!!!!

I don't know what the other tasks are yet. I'm only allowed to do one a day.

Sam put down his pen. The ancient scroll was beside him, but he'd promised Prune that he wouldn't so much as peep at it until they were alone together.

So far, the day had been a disaster. Prune's music teacher had arrived just as they were plotting their escape after breakfast, and Sam had spent most of the morning listening to his cousin trying to play the Mothscale national anthem on the bagpipes. As Prune could only play two notes, the wails and screeches were horrendous. Sam was finally rescued by Uncle Archibald coming out of his office with tufts of cotton wool stuffed in his ears, insisting that the lesson was continued elsewhere. Preferably in Australia, but the garden room would do.

The sound of wheels on the cobbles made Sam look out of the window.

"I expect that's the music teacher leaving," he said to the doodlebird. "Yes … there he goes. He doesn't look very happy. Still, he's gone, and now Prune and I can get on with the second task!"

NO MILK
TODAY

Tingalinga bang bang bang!!!!!

It was the bell for lunch.

"Hurrah!" Sam jumped up and headed for the door. He leapt down the stairs three at a time and skidded into the dining room, only to find he was the first one there.

Aunt Eglantine, coming in shortly afterwards, gave him a brisk nod. "Glad to see that you're punctual for once, Sam." She sat herself at the head of the table, and looked round.

"I don't, however, see Prunella. Do you know where she is?"

"No, Aunt Egg." Sam shook his head.

His aunt helped herself to several large spoonfuls of fish pie. "Prunella is late. I am ALWAYS on time, despite my MANY responsibilities. If the Duchess of Mothscale can arrive at the dining table on the stroke of one o'clock, I completely fail to see why Prunella cannot do the same."

"Sorry, Aunt Egg," Sam apologised. When Aunt Egg was in a bad mood it was best to be as polite as possible.

His aunt heaved a gusty sigh. "I despair of you young things. Kindly pass the carrots."

"Yes, Aunt Egg." Sam got up and fetched the carrots from the other end of the table. As he did so, Uncle Archibald came marching in. He winked at Sam before piling his plate with

fish pie and settling down to eat.

"REALLY, Archie!" Aunt Egg frowned.
"MUST you wink at the boy? His manners are
bad enough, without you encouraging him.
Only ploughboys wink!"

"Ploughboy?" Uncle Archibald looked
round. "What's that? Sam taken up ploughing?
Jolly hard work, my lad. No, no. Don't you

bother with that kind of thing. I say, Eglantine old bean – this pie's a bit dry, what what what. Cook having a day off?"

Aunt Egg gave her husband a chilly look. "If you are suggesting that I made the pie, Archibald, the answer is no. Cook made it. Unfortunately there was no milk delivery this morni—"

The dining room door opened with a crash, and Prune appeared, scowling.

Her mother pointed at the clock. "Prunella! You're late!"

"It's not MY fault," Prune said. "I had to put my bagpipes away. Stupid things. Can't I play the trumpet instead? I'd be much better at playing the trumpet than the bagpipes, you know."

Uncle Archibald raised a bristly eyebrow. "The trumpet, eh? Tantarra! Tantarra, and all that. Very fine instrument! Just the thing to open a tournament. Why, I remember—" He caught Aunt Egg's frosty expression, and stopped.

"We've discussed this before," Aunt Egg said coldly. "The trumpet is not a suitable instrument for a young lady."

"Mr McWhisker says I don't suit the bagpipes." Prune peered at the fish pie. "This looks horrid. Isn't there any parsley sauce?"

"The milk cart didn't arrive this morning." Aunt Egg sounded even more annoyed. "I shall have to tell Farmer Mole that I am not at all happy. If he isn't here by teatime there will be serious consequences. EXTREMELY serious consequences! Now, eat up. I've got a delightful afternoon planned for you and Sam – although I'm not sure that you deserve it!"

Prune and Sam exchanged glances. What about the scroll? And the second task?

"But, Ma—" Prune began.

Aunt Egg interrupted her. "Don't you *but, Ma* me, young lady! Just listen. First of all, I want you and Sam to take Horace back to his owner. Of course, I don't usually deliver, but Lord Scratch is a valuable customer, and I want to keep him happy. Just make sure that Horace doesn't get dirty.

20

There is to be NO ROLLING IN THE MUD!"

Sam's heart sank into his boots. Aunt Egg offered Luxury Accommodation for Dragons, Griffins and Other Regal Beasts in order to pay the expenses of Mothscale Castle. Most of her guests were hairy or scaly, and very self-opinionated. Horace the warthog was no different.

Prune was glaring at her mother. "But, MA! We CAN'T! Scratch Castle is MILES away! It'll take us AGES!"

"But you don't have to go to the castle, Prunella!" Aunt Egg glared back at her daughter. "Lord Scratch is going to meet you at Weasel's Hill!"

"Weasel's Hill?" Uncle Archibald stopped pushing fish pie round his plate with his fork and looked interested. "County fair, is it?"

Sam and Prune sat up. A county fair

sounded fun … But Aunt Egg shook her head and they slumped back into their chairs.

"Not the county fair, Archie. That was last month. But it's the annual cabbage-throwing competition, and Lord Scratch is one of the judges." She gave Sam a hearty slap on the

back that sent him face first into his carrots. "So there you are, Sam! A delightful afternoon, and I hope you'll appreciate it, even if my daughter is determined not to."

"Don't be so mean, Ma," Prune said. "You never said anything about a competition. That sounds jolly. Can we throw cabbages too?"

Aunt Egg looked disapproving. "I don't think that would be suitable," she began, but Uncle Archibald dug in his pockets, and produced a couple of coins.

"Here, Prune m'dear – one for you, and one for the boy. Used to be a penny a cabbage in my day. See what you can win."

"Thanks, Pa!" Prune handed Sam a penny. "Do they have prizes, then?"

Her father nodded. "Sure to. Chap who

throws the cabbage the furthest wins. Scratch always donates a pig. There'll be other things as well, I expect. Flowery teacloths, or something of the sort."

"Thank you VERY much, sir." Sam smiled at his uncle. "Would you like the pig if we win it?"

"Certainly not!" Aunt Egg was emphatic. "We offer Luxury Accommodation for Regal Beasts, not common pigs. On the other hand …" A thoughtful look crossed her face. "A flowery teacloth might come in useful …"

Uncle Archibald got up from the table. "Let the children win something for themselves," he said. "Always fun, winning things." He gazed into space. "I remember a joust, many years ago—"

"No time for that, Archibald!" Aunt Egg tapped the table with a spoon and, much to

Sam's disappointment,
Uncle Archibald
wandered away without
finishing his story.

"I do wish Aunt Egg
wasn't quite so bossy," Sam
thought sadly. He was
certain his uncle
had a store of
information about
knights and
adventures and
Noble Deeds, but
Aunt Egg always
refused to let her
husband talk about
his past. "We must
look to the future!"
was her motto.

Sam sighed, and went back to his dry fish pie. When were he and Prune going to get a chance to find out what  the next task was? When was he going to be able to begin Noble Deeds of his own?

"If I collect the scroll before we go out," he thought, "Prune and I can do what it says later on this afternoon—"

"Stop playing with your food, Sam!" Aunt Egg whisked his plate away. "And you've finished too, Prunella. Come along! It's a lovely day. You don't need coats." And Sam and Prune were hustled into the front courtyard, where an elderly warthog was grubbing up yellow tulips.

"Oh, Horace! You naughty, naughty boy!"

Aunt Egg wagged her finger at the warthog, who took no notice. "Now, Prunella and Sam are here to take you back to Daddy! Won't that be nice?"

Horace looked first at Prune, then at Sam, and his ears flattened.

"That'll be a no," Prune said, under her breath.

"What a funny boy you are, Horace!" Aunt Egg undid the warthog's golden chain and handed it to her daughter. "Prunella – you're to go along Drover's Road. Under no circumstances are you to go down Folly Lane, do you hear? It'll be nothing but puddles. I don't want Horace going back to Lord Scratch covered in mud."

"Yes, Ma. Whatever you say, Ma." Prune rolled her eyes at Sam. "We'll go along Drover's Road, Ma."

"Really, Princess Prunella!" Aunt Egg snapped. "I've a good mind to send you to your room for the rest of the day! Whatever's the matter with you?"

Prune made a face. "It's playing the bagpipes. It makes me cross. I'd be SO much nicer if I played the trumpet."

Her mother folded her arms. "Being rude and unpleasant to your mother is no way to get what you want, young lady."

"Oh!" Prune smiled a huge smile. "So if I'm sweet and good you WILL let me?" She flung her arms round her mother and hugged her. "DARLING Ma! I'll be sweet and good all day today! I promise! And tomorrow I'll start the trumpet. Come on, Sam! Let's get going!"

Aunt Egg, not wishing to admit she had been tricked, turned hastily to Sam. "Have you been paying attention, Sam?"

Sam nodded. "Yes, Aunt Egg. Drover's Road. No puddles."

"Good. And remember – if I hear there's been any trouble there will be NO trumpet lessons!" And Aunt Egg sailed away before Prune could have the last word.

THE ROYAL WARTHOG

Horace, Prune and Sam inspected each other.

"I thought royal warthogs were noble beasts," Sam said doubtfully. "Horace doesn't exactly look noble to me. More … grumpy."

Horace glared at him.

"Ma's always giving him baths," Prune said, "and I don't think he likes them much. Hey – have you got the scroll?"

Sam shook his head, and Prune looked at him in surprise. "Why ever not?"

"I was going to get it after lunch," Sam told her, "but we got thrown out of the castle."

"So today's going to be a total waste of time." Prune frowned. "I thought you wanted to be a Very Noble Knight more than anything, Sam. You'll never get to be a knight if you don't get on with the tasks."

"I know," Sam agreed, but then he brightened. "Hey! I'll get Dandy to fetch it for us!" And he whistled loudly.

A moment later the doodlebird flew down, already carrying the scroll in his claws.

"Thanks, Dandy!" Sam took the precious scroll.

"How did you know that was what I wanted?"

Dandy looked pleased with himself. "A𝗪𝗞!"

He gave the warthog a suspicious look. "A𝗪𝗞?"

"We've got to take him back to his owner," Sam explained. "He belongs to Lord Scratch. He's called—"

"Never mind about Horace," Prune interrupted. "What does the scroll say? What do we have to do next?"

Holding his breath, Sam unrolled the list of tasks. The last time he and Prune had seen it the letters had been gleaming gold. Now they were black, and difficult to read.

"Thou shalt be … what's the next word?" Sam squinted at the scroll. "I can't make it out."

"Me neither," Prune said. "But I bet it's something really boring like *be patient*." A brief flicker crossed the parchment, and Prune sighed heavily. "See? It was agreeing with me."

Sam traced the letters with his finger, then jumped. "OUCH! It's HOT!"

Prune leant forward. "Let's see ... Look! It's turning gold!"

"YES!" Sam punched the air. "It's the next task!"

Together he and Prune read,

"*Task two: Thou shalt not seek out a snow-white steed.*"

"What?" Sam's excitement drained away.

He wanted a snow white-steed more than anything. How could he possibly be a Very Noble Knight without one?

"Hang on a minute," Prune told him. "There's a bit more. *Thou shalt not seek out a snow-white steed, but must gain it by thy Noble Deeds*. What does that mean?"

Sam scratched his head. "We've got to find a white horse – but we can't go looking for it. We have to do Noble Deeds, and sort of win it. Like a swap. At least, I think that's what it means ... I do wish it were clearer!"

He rolled the scroll up again, and stuffed it in his pocket. "We'll have to have another look later. Going to a cabbage-throwing competition may be fun, but it isn't exactly a Noble Deed, is it." He paused. "Do you think taking a grumpy warthog back to his owner might count? Just a little bit?"

Horace snorted, stood up on his hindlegs, and gave Sam a sharp push. Sam staggered, slipped and sat down with a bump. Prune laughed, Horace's piggy little eyes gleamed, and even the doodlebird hid a chuckle.

"That's not funny," Sam complained as he got to his feet.

"Serves you right," Prune said. "You shouldn't call him names. But we'd better get going." Horace grunted, and Prune gave his chain an encouraging shake. "Are you ready, Mr Warthog? Let's get you home for tea!"

"OINK!" Horace set off at a gallop, towing Prune behind him.

"WHEEEE!" she yelled. "Go, Horace! Go!"

Sam, taken by surprise, was left standing. "Wait for me!" he shouted. As he chased after his cousin, the doodlebird flew above, squawking encouragingly.

On and on they went,
down the drive, past a
signpost pointing to Drover's
Road, and then, with a loud "Whoop!" Prune
made a sharp right turn. As she sprinted up
the narrow muddy lane, Sam, already out of
breath, doubled up with a stitch in his side.

"Prune!" he yelled. "Prune! Stop!"

Prune, with some difficulty, persuaded
Horace to slow to a walk and Sam, puffing
hard, caught up with them. "You were
running too fast," he said. "I got a stitch."

"It was Horace's fault." Prune was only
mildly apologetic. "He wants to get home." She
considered her red-faced cousin. "You need to
take more exercise, you know. I'm sure Very
Noble Knights should be able to run for miles."

Horace nodded his huge hairy head and
Sam, still panting, frowned. "When I get my

snow-white steed," he said, "I won't need to run for miles."

Prune raised her eyebrows. "Oh yes? And where are you going to get this horse from? I haven't noticed you doing any Noble Deeds in the last ten minutes."

"I don't know," Sam admitted. "But I'll find one somehow. And why didn't we go along Drover's Road like your mother said?"

His cousin grinned. "Did you really think I was going to take the long way round? I want to get to Weasel's Hill and have a go at cabbage throwing. It's tons quicker this way! Just make sure nobody notices us when we go through Weasel Village. We don't want Ma to find out we didn't do as she said – not when I've finally got her to agree to trumpet lessons."

Before Sam could answer, the doodlebird gave a warning squawk. A flock of sheep was rushing towards them, their eyes popping.

"Quick! Get out of the way!" Sam shouted, but Horace was already scrambling up the bank, Prune close behind him. They were just in time – the sheep dashed past them in a white woolly stream, bleating wildly as they went.

"What's the matter with them?" Sam asked.

"AWK AWK," said the doodlebird.

Sam peered at him. "They saw WHAT?"

The doodlebird shrugged. "AK."

"WOW!" Sam squinted up the lane in the direction the sheep had come from. "Dandy says they saw a tree in the middle of the village, where there's never been one before, and it whistled at them!"

"A tree?" Prune handed Horace's chain to Sam so she could jump down the muddy bank. "In the village?"

Sam nodded. "And it wasn't there yesterday."

"That's exciting!" Prune was thrilled. "I've heard about walking trees, but I've never ever seen one. Let's go and have a look."

"OK," Sam said. "Come on, Horace."

Horace didn't move.

He was inspecting the mud with a thoughtful gleam in his eye.

"Oh – PLEASE don't roll!" Sam begged. "Aunt Egg'll be furious!"

Horace grunted his opinion of Aunt Egg, and lay down.

Prune turned round to see what was going on. "What are you doing? Hurry up – don't you want to see a walking tree?"

"Horace wants to roll in the mud," Sam explained. He stared down at the solid body of the warthog, and Horace stared back. With a sigh, Sam gave in. "Look here, Horace. If I let you have a good roll, will you come with us?"

Horace said nothing, but his bristles sank down and a friendlier expression came over his face.

"OK." Sam nodded. "Get rolling."

Horace gave a grunt that was almost cheerful, and proceeded to roll in an  exceptionally thorough manner. Once he had finished he shook himself, sending spatters of mud in all directions, and allowed Sam to lead him to where Prune was waiting.

Prune giggled when she saw the mud-covered animal. "Looks as if he enjoyed that," she said. "Ma insisted on  giving him a rose-scented bubble bath every morning AND every evening!"

Sam gave Horace a sympathetic grin. "No wonder you were grumpy." Horace skipped a couple of small skips, and Sam turned to Prune. "Who told you about walking trees? I don't think they walk anywhere near where I live."

"Pa told me." Prune lowered her voice, even though her mother was a long way away. "He told me a story once about a tree that helped him trip up a troll. Ma was really cross and said I wasn't to believe a word of it, but I do."

"I do too." Sam nodded. "A tree waved at me last night, and when I waved back, it waved again from a different place."

Prune's eyes widened. "Really?" Then, not wanting Sam to see she was impressed, she added, "It could easily have been two different trees. Let's get going!"

As the party set off, Sam was aware of a

growing feeling of excitement. Uncle Archibald knew about walking trees, and Uncle Archibald was a knight. Maybe this was a sign that something knightly lay ahead? After all, once he and Prune had delivered Horace and had tried throwing cabbages, they could begin their Noble Deeds ... and then, at last, he might find his snow-white steed.

WHAT'S THE PLAN?

As they drew nearer to the village, the doodlebird, who was perched on Sam's shoulder, suddenly stretched his wings and flew up in the air. "Awk!"

"What's he saying?" Prune asked.

"He says someone's coming," Sam replied.

As Dandy settled down again, a small boy came running along the lane towards them. "You don't want to go up there," he gasped.

"There's a horrible old tree throwing hazelnuts all over the place!" And he dashed past them.

"WOW!" Sam said, and Prune tugged at Horace's chain. "Hey, Horace! If we hurry up you might find some hazelnuts!"

A moment later a nut flew over the hedge bordering the lane, and hit Horace on the nose. He grunted, and ate it with much enthusiastic crunching. It was followed by several others, and the warthog pranced

from one side of the lane to the other, eating the nuts as they fell.

"It's a shame he can't catch them," Prune said as she tried to dodge a new flurry. "OUCH! They sting!"

"Awk," said the doodlebird, "Awk?"

Prune looked up. "What's he saying?"

"He's wondering if we should take Horace into the village," Sam translated.

"Oh …" Prune considered. "He could be right. Someone might recognise him, and tell Ma. But we can't leave him here, can we?"

"Dandy could keep an eye on him," Sam suggested. "And he's very happy eating hazelnuts. There are loads here."

This was true. Horace had every appearance of a blissfully happy warthog. Sam unfastened the gold chain to set him free, and went on, "Dandy'll find us if anything goes wrong."

Prune hesitated. "I suppose it'll be OK," she said. "Horace! You won't run away, will you?"

The warthog shook his heavy head with a loud grunt.

"AWK," the doodlebird said, and Sam laughed.

"Dandy says Horace won't move until he's eaten all the hazelnuts."

"Good," Prune said, and she and Sam hurried down the lane, dodging hazelnuts as best they could. Before too long they rounded a corner, and there was the village in front of them.

And so was the tree.

Sam looked, blinked, and looked again. Folly Lane ended at a T-junction, and in the middle, blocking the road completely, was a knobbly hazel tree hurling hazelnuts in all directions.

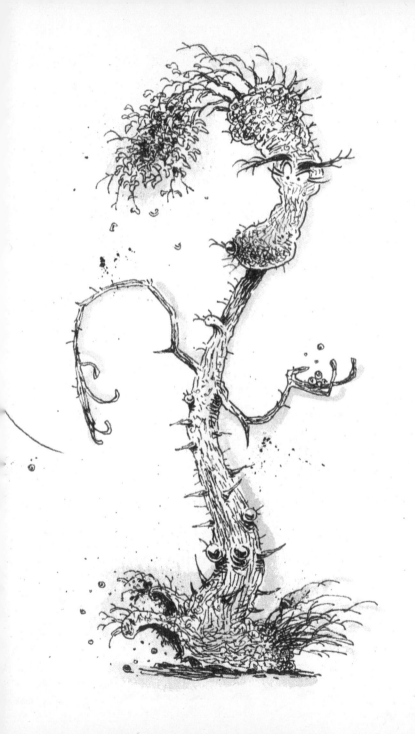

Villagers were ducking as the nuts hailed down and shouting at the tree to behave itself. The tree was taking no notice.

Trying not to draw attention to themselves, Sam and Prune edged towards it to have a better look. "Wow!" Sam whispered. "Wow wow WOWSERS!"

Prune crept another step nearer. "Pa was right!" A hazelnut hit her on the forehead, and she squealed indignantly. "Oops!" She clapped a hand over her mouth, but it was too late. An old man had heard her, and he swung round.

"Why! If it isn't the duke's kid! Look, Betty!"

A large woman carrying a basket stared, then dropped a clumsy curtsey. "Thank goodness you're here, your ladyship! Come on behalf of your dad, have you? You and your friend?"

She put down the basket and clapped her hands. "Look who's here! The duke's sent his daughter!"

"About time too," grumbled a red-faced farmer. "I can't get my milk cart past that tree, and I've deliveries to make. Should have been at the castle hours ago."

Another farmer glared at him. "You think you've got problems, Jim Mole? I can't move my wagon, and I need to be at Weasel's Hill! Promised his lordship I'd be there by twelve, didn't I, and twelve's long gone!"

"Stop moaning, Joe." The large woman shook her head. "They're here now, aren't they? Her ladyship'll know what to do, won't you, ducks?"

"A ladyship? Has she come to help?" Another woman came hurrying up, and within seconds a small crowd had gathered around Prune and Sam. Even the hazel tree stopped throwing nuts, and leant over to see what was going on.

"Erm ..."
Prune began,
then stopped
and looked at
Sam. "What do I
say?" she whispered.

Sam gulped. Should a knight-in-training be able to deal with a runaway tree? "Say ... say

we've come to see what's going
on, so we can make a plan."

Prune stood up very straight. "Ladies,
gentlemen and … and tree. We've come to –
erm – check out the situation."

The crowd nodded, and waited for more.
Prune nudged Sam. "Your turn," she hissed.

Sam pointed at the tree. "Tree? Ahem. I am
Sam J. Butterbiggins, knight-in-training, and
this is my True Companion, the Lady Prunella
of Mothscale Castle. Please explain what you're
doing here."

The tree waved a branch in greeting.
"Bored," it said, in a high-pitched squeak.
"Bored. Boring forest. Nothing to see.
No fun."

"Oh." Sam wasn't sure how to answer this.
"Well … you can't stay here, you know."

"That's right," Prune agreed. "And why are

you throwing hazelnuts at everyone?"

"Silly people," the tree squeaked. "Silly people fetched an axe. Hazel doesn't like axes."

Sam stared. "Who's Hazel?"

The tree threw a well-aimed nut and hit Sam on the nose. "Me is Hazel! Silly boy!"

"Ouch!" Sam's eyes were watering. "So you came here because you were bored?"

"Yuss," said the tree, and it drooped. "Poor Hazel. Nobody loves Hazel."

The red-faced Farmer Mole pushed his way forward. "Excuse me, young sir and miss, but all this chit-chat isn't getting my milk cart to the castle. The duchess, she's a terror for punctuality. I'll lose my job if I don't get there soon!"

"You'll lose your job?" Joe folded his arms. "If I don't get my cabbages to Weasel's Hill I'll lose everything! I've got twelve boxes for the competition, and you can't throw cabbages if you don't have cabbages to throw."

"I'm going to that," said a tall girl. "I want to win the chickens!"

At once other voices joined in. "I want to win a big pork pie!"

"I wants a cheese!"

"I know what I want," said a small boy with very bright blue eyes. "There's a fat little pig as a prize, and I really, really, REALLY want to win that!"

"You won't be winning anything, Bobby, if I don't get those cabbages to Weasel's Hill," Joe said gloomily. "And nor will anyone else."

The villagers surged closer to Sam and Prune. "So when's this tree going to be moved, then?"

"Come on, knight-in-training! What's the plan?"

"How's Joe going to get his cabbages to Weasel's Hill?"

The large woman with the basket held up her hand. "Hush! Let's hear what Miss Prunella and the lad have to say!"

There was a sudden silence, and all eyes turned to Prune and Sam.

CABBAGES AND MILK

Sam swallowed hard. His stomach felt as if it was full of butterflies. The crowd began to shift impatiently, and Sam felt his butterflies loop and circle. "I bet there's nothing in the scroll about this," he thought. "I'm sure rescuing princesses from monsters is easier than sorting out milk and cabbages—"

PING!!!

An idea hit him.

He took a step forward, and held up his hand.

"Excuse me," he said, "but I've just thought of something." He turned to Farmer Mole. "You need to get to the palace, and Mr Joe wants to go the other way, to Weasel's Hill. Your wagon's on one side of the tree, and his cart's on the other – so why don't you just swap the milk and cabbages?"

There was a long pause.

Farmer Mole was the first to break the silence. "So ..." he said slowly, "I put my milk churns on Joe's wagon?"

Sam smiled encouragingly.

"And then I take Joe's horses and drive his wagon to the castle to deliver the milk?"

Prune gave Farmer Mole a thumbs up. "That's right!"

"While I put my cabbages on Mole's cart …" Joe was rubbing at his chin. "And take his cart to Weasel's Hill. H'm. What do you think, Mole?"

"Sounds good to me," Farmer Mole said.

"Me too," said Joe.

The villagers gave a ragged cheer, and Prune banged Sam on the back. "You're not as stupid as you look, Sam J. Butterbiggins," she said.

Farmer Mole came closer. "If it hadn't been for you, young sir and miss, I'd have lost my job. Clever, that's what you are – and I'll make sure I tell the duchess."

"NO! I mean …" Prune shook her head. "Erm … that's very kind of you, but don't tell anyone!"

The farmer looked puzzled. "But I'll need to say about the tree, miss. We can't have it blocking the road, and the duke's the man to sort it out, him being our landlord and all."

"But WE'VE come to sort it out!" Sam hoped he sounded more confident than he felt. "That's why we're here, isn't it, Prune – I mean, Prunella? It'll be gone by the time you get back from the palace. Truly!"

"All gone," Prune promised.

"Well ..." Farmer Mole hesitated. "I'll not mention it, then. Can't say I mind – means I can deliver the churns and get to the competition before it's all over. The road'll be clear by the time I get back, you say?"

"Yes." Prune had her fingers crossed behind her back.

"Then that's sorted." The farmer turned to the watching villagers. "Come on, folks – lend a hand!" and he hurried off to bring his wagon as close to the tree as possible. Joe did the same from the other side, and a moment later the exchange of milk churns for boxes of cabbages was under way.

Prune ran to help, but Sam stood gazing at Joe's horses. One was brown ... but the other was snow white.

"A snow-white steed," he whispered. "A real snow-white steed!"

"Come on, Sam!" Prune shouted, and Sam slowly went to join her. This was a farmer's horse, he told himself. It belonged to Joe. There was no way it could be the horse of his dreams.

With a sigh Sam helped load the last milk churn, and in a matter of minutes the white horse and its brown companion were trotting away in the direction of Mothscale Castle.

Joe had taken a little longer to make sure his cabbages were safely stacked. As he swung himself up on to Farmer Mole's cart, he nodded to Prune. "I'm not a man for flowery speeches," he said, "but you've saved me a heap of trouble. Anything I can do for you young 'uns, you let old Joe Lumpkin know."

Prune glanced at Sam, but he was still looking longingly after the disappearing wagon. "I don't suppose you'd like to give Sam your white horse, would you? It sounds a bit rude, but I'm his True Companion, and I'm supposed to look out for him."

Joe took off his hat, scratched his head, and put the hat back on again. "My white horse?

71

She's not for sale, your ladyship. I need two
to pull my old wagon, see. But I'll keep an eye
out for you, and that's for sure." And with an
encouraging "Giddy up!" he turned Farmer
Mole's cart round and headed off towards
Weasel's Hill.

"Hurrah! There's going to be a competition
after all! I'm off to win the
pig!" said a girl.

"No you're not! I'M going to win it!" Bobby told her. "I really, really, REALLY want it!"

"And I want the chickens …"

"And I want the cheese …"

"Let's go!"

The chorus of voices faded as the villagers tramped away to Weasel's Hill. Two minutes later Sam and Prune were almost alone. Only two old men were left, leaning on their sticks and waiting to see what would happen next.

Prune went back to the tree. It was still
drooping, but she had the feeling it had been
paying close attention to everything that had
been going on. Sam came to stand beside her,
and together they looked up into the branches.

"Mrs Tree," Sam said. "If we asked you nicely, would you move?"

The tree flicked Sam's nose with a twiggy finger. "No!"

"But you're causing loads of trouble!" Sam was indignant, but Prune took his arm and pulled him away.

"Shh," she whispered. "We've got to be clever, or it'll never move! And we've absolutely got to make it go away, because if we don't then Ma'll find out we didn't do as she told us – and I can't BEAR the thought of another bagpipe lesson."

Sam wasn't sure he could bear another bagpipe lesson either. He was also worried about Aunt Egg. When Aunt Egg was angry, she was scary. VERY scary.

"OK." He glanced back at the tree. "What should we do?"

"H'm." Prune was thinking. "If I want Ma
to do something, I always say I know she can't
possibly do it, and then she does it just to
prove she can. It might just work!" She nudged
Sam. "Make sure you agree with me …" Then,
raising her voice so the tree was sure to hear,

she went on, "It's no good. This tree isn't going to move. It's here for keeps. I know you think it's silly, Sam, but there you are … trees ARE silly. There's a lovely village green just over there, where it could put down its roots and be comfortable, but it'll never think of that. Never."

Sam was trying not to laugh. "Oh, yes!" he said. "I see what you mean. SUCH a lovely village green! But you're right. Trees are silly!"

There was a rustling in the branches above their heads, but the tree said nothing.

Prune tried again. "So you see, Sam, it's no good trying to talk to it. It won't listen. And it CERTAINLY won't move!"

"Biddly biddly boo!" the tree squeaked. "NOT silly! If Hazel wants to sit on village green, Hazel will. Watch me, kiddy widdies! Hazel moooooooooving …"

There was more rustling, and creaking. Sam and Prune held their breath …

And then came a loud cackle of laughter.

"Tee-hee hee hee! Hazel tricked you, kiddy widdies! Not moving – not ever!"

The triumphant smile on Prune's face vanished. "Sam!" she hissed. "Think of something!"

Sam's head was whirling – but a picture suddenly flashed into his mind. Horace! Horace digging up Aunt Egg's tulips! Was it worth a try?

He set off at a run …
and all but bumped
into Horace and the
doodlebird coming out
of Folly Lane.

The doodlebird
greeted Sam with a cheery
"AWK!" and waved a wing at Horace. "AWK."

"He's eaten all the hazelnuts?" Sam said.
"And he's still hungry? Good! I've got a job for
him to do!"

Horace looked up hopefully, and Sam bent
down to whisper in his ear. "You see this tree?
It's got LOADS of nuts all round its roots …"

The warthog gave a grunt, and headed
for the tree with a gleam in his eyes. The tree
saw him coming, and let out a shriek. Horace
snorted, and a moment later was digging
enthusiastically.

"Hiddle hiddle biddle biddle hic hic hic …"

Sam and Prune stared. It was the tree – but what was it doing?

"Hic hic hiddle hiddle HIC!"

Prune began to laugh. "Horace is tickling it – and it doesn't like it!"

"Get off!" The tree was waving its branches wildly.

"Get away from Hazel! Nasty piggy wiggy! Shoo! Shoo! SHOOOOOO!"

Horace took no notice. With a final "HIC!"
the tree shivered, staggered, and began to
move. Grumbling and mumbling to itself, it
hooked its longest roots over a low branch,
and swayed its way off the road and on to the
village green. There
it heaved a sigh,
and settled into
the grass.

"Hazel tired,"
it announced.
"Hazel go to
sleep now. Don't
disturb."

Horace stayed where he was, hazelnuts all around him. As far as he was concerned, food was what mattered, not trees.

"WOW!" Sam and Prune looked at each other in delight, while the two old villagers inspected the hazel tree.

"Nice to have a bit of shade," one remarked.

"That's right," said another. "And the nuts will come in handy. Long as it doesn't start throwing them round again, of course."

The tree opened one eye. "No axes?"

"Not as long as you stay where you are," Sam called.

"Then no throwing," the tree promised. "Now hush, kiddy widdies. Hazel sleeping."

A SNOW-WHITE STEED

It was almost as hard to persuade Horace to move as it had been to move the tree. In the end, Prune scooped up as many nuts as she could carry, and every ten metres or so, dropped a handful on the side of the road. The warthog snuffled his way after her, grunting a complaint if he felt he hadn't had enough.

It was lucky that Weasel's Hill wasn't far, and that the slope wasn't too steep – by the time they had puffed their way up to the top there were very few nuts left.

"Sam!" Prune pointed. "There's Joe!"

Sam looked where she was pointing, and saw Joe loading empty boxes on to Farmer Mole's cart. Cabbages were heaped behind a white line painted on the grass, and a girl was collecting pennies as villagers came to choose their missile for the first throw of the competition.

"Penny a cabbage!" she said. "First throw's for the pig! Next throw'll be for the chickens, and after that it's for pork pies and cheeses."

"Let's try for the pig," Prune said. "Which cabbage do you want, Sam?"

"I don't know." Sam wasn't sure he wanted to try to win a pig. If the prize had been a snow-white steed, it would have been very

different. He was beginning to wonder if he and Prune would ever be able to go and find someone who needed a Noble Deed doing. If they didn't, would that mean they'd lost their chance?

He picked up the nearest cabbage and handed the girl his penny. Prune took longer choosing hers, and by the time she had decided, Joe had finished tidying his boxes and a row of villagers had taken their places behind the white line. At the bottom of the hill was another line, and Sam could see a bespectacled man standing behind it. In one hand he was holding a piece of rope, and on the end of the rope was a pig. In his other hand was a whistle.

Bobby, the small boy with the very blue eyes, nudged Sam. "You did ought to get ready," he said. "His lordship – that's him in the glasses, 'n' he's the judge – he'll blow his whistle any minute now, and that's when we throw the cabbages!"

Prune had already taken her place. Sam made his way to join her, and she looked at him in surprise. "What's the matter with you? You look like a wet lettuce!"

"I just want to get on with the next task," Sam said. "It's all very well sorting out trees and throwing cabbages around, but I do SO want a horse. The scroll said we should do

Noble Deeds, and we haven't even started."

"But, Sam! We've done at least—"

Prune was interrupted by a piercing blast from the whistle. The villagers stepped forward, and with shouts of encouragement from all sides, hurled their cabbages down the hill. Sam, sighing heavily, was about to toss his cabbage after them when Horace spotted Lord Scratch. The warthog leapt forward with a snort of delight at seeing his owner.

As he did so, he knocked into Sam's
arm, and the cabbage sailed up into
the air. Up and up it flew, then
curved in a downwards arc to land
several metres beyond the white line.

"The winner!" shouted Lord Scratch.
"A clear winner!"

A moment later, Horace arrived at full
speed, and Lord Scratch disappeared under
the full weight of a loving warthog. He
struggled out a moment later, waving Sam's
cabbage. "The winner!" he called. "Who's the
lucky winner of the pig?"

"It's him!" Bobby pointed to Sam. "He won
it." Bobby sniffed, and wiped his eyes

with a grubby hand. "He won the pig, he did."

Sam looked at the small boy. "But I didn't mean to … I really didn't."

Bobby sniffed again. "Don't matter. You won it, fair and square."

Sam made a decision. "Tell you what. YOU have it! I know you really, really wanted that pig, so I'll give it to you. Come on – let's go and collect it." And Sam, the astonished Bobby, and Prune made their way down the hill.

At the bottom, Lord Scratch was waiting, and he beamed when he saw Prune. "Prunella! Well done!"

"What for? I didn't do anything," Prune said.

"Horace is looking better than ever," Lord

Scratch told her. "Delighted! Delighted! Last time, he came back smelling of roses. Not the thing at all. And who's this? The winner of the pig?"

Sam made his best bow. "Sam J. Butterbiggins, sir," he said. "And if you don't mind, could I give the pig to my friend Bobby?" He pushed the small boy forward.

"Give Bobby the pig? Of course, of course. Kind of you, Sam J. Butterbiggins. Very kind." Lord Scratch handed the rope to Bobby. "Look after it, laddie!"

Bobby, quite unable to speak, nodded, his blue eyes sparkling.

"It's not really kind," Sam said. "I didn't mean to win it, you see. If anything, Horace won it."

"Clever chap, my Horace." Lord Scratch patted the warthog's bristly head, then turned

back to Sam and Prune. "But Farmer Joe tells
me that you're not so silly yourselves. Saved
the day, the two of you! Found a way to get
the cabbages safely here! Now that's a good
deed, and I thank you for it. Couldn't have
had a competition without those cabbages,
you know."

Prune stuck
her finger in
Sam's chest.
"THAT'S what I
was about to tell
you, stupid Sam!
You've been going
on and on about
not being able to do
Noble Deeds, but we've ALREADY done one!"

"Oh." Sam blinked. "Have we?"

"Yes," Prune said firmly. "AND we moved
the tree! So that's TWO!"

The doodlebird, landing on Sam's shoulder,
nibbled his ear fondly. "AWK."

"Ahem!" Joe had
come up silently, and was
standing right behind
them. "I'd say it was three,

young sir. Our Bobby's been pining for that pig for weeks and weeks. He's my daughter's boy, and we've heard nothing but pig pig pig ever since the competition was announced." Joe coughed again. "Now, like I said, I'm not one for speeches – but Lady Prunella here, she told me how you were wanting a white horse. Well, when I was driving Farmer Mole's little cart along the road I was thinking, this is a fine way to drive! A little cart and a single horse makes things ever so easy. My old wagon, well – she takes two horses, and that's an extra horse eating its head off in hay all year round. So, I'm swapping my wagon for a cart soon as I can, and if you'd like my Dora – well, you're welcome to her."

It was Sam's turn to be lost for words.

Prune answered for him. "He says yes, Mr Joe, and he says thank you very much indeed."

Joe nodded. "Then that's settled. And if I'm not much mistaken, that's Mole bringing my wagon back along the road. Saxon can pull it home on his own – so if you want old Dora, you can have her right now."

Sam stared at him. Did the farmer mean it?

Prune stuck her elbow into her cousin's side. "Oi! Sam! You look just like a goldfish. Say thank you, and let's get home before Ma sends out a search party."

"Oh ... yes." Sam's face was one enormous smile. "Thank you, thank you, THANK YOU Mr Joe!"

This has been the very very VERY best day of my life! I've done my second task! Dora is in the stable next to Prune's pony, and tomorrow Prune and I are going to go out riding together because I've got my very own snow-white steed AT LAST!

I thought it would be difficult explaining how I got Dora to Aunt Egg, but she thought I'd won her in the competition and Prune said not to tell her that it wasn't QUITE like that. So I didn't.

Prune has her first ever trumpet lesson tomorrow, so she's very happy. Aunt Egg is happy too, because the milk finally arrived, and Cook made a rice pudding for supper (yuck!) which is Aunt Egg's favourite.

Uncle Archibald is happy because Aunt Egg is happy, and I'm the happiest of them all ... And tomorrow, we'll see what the scroll says for the third task. I don't mind what it is, though. I've got Dora. And with a snow—white steed I can do ANYTHING!

Join Sam and Prune
on their third quest!

KNIGHT
IN TRAINING

A VERY
BOTHERSOME BEAR

Read on for a sneak peek …

**Hodder
Children's
Books**

A division of Hachette Children's Group

A Very Early Start

Dear diary,

It's VERY early in the morning, but I'm much too excited to sleep.

Guess what? I've got my very own snow-white steed! A snow-white steed is EXACTLY what Very Noble Knights always ride, and I want to be a Very Noble Knight who does Noble Deeds more than anything else in the world.

Sam closed his diary, and looked across his bedroom to where the doodlebird was fast asleep.

"What's the time, Dandy? Is it time to get up yet?"

The doodlebird woke with a jump. "AWK!" Then, making his point even more firmly, he tucked his head back under his wing and began to snore.

Sam sighed, and reached for his pen.

I'm on my way to being a knight. My True Companion (that's my cousin Prune) and I found an ancient scroll, and it tells us what to do. It's magic — the letters glow gold! And they get quite hot as well. Prune's looking after the scroll at the moment. I hope she's being really, really careful with it. We can't tell Aunt Egg what we're doing, because she doesn't like it AT ALL when Uncle Archibald tells stories about when he was young and was a Very Noble Knight. Aunt Egg is quite strict. I expect that's why Prune is sometimes annoying.

Sam stopped, and looked at what he had written. Was he being fair to Prune? He decided he was, and went on.

But, I don't mind staying here with Aunt Egg and Uncle Archibald while Mother and Father are away. I didn't like it when I first got to Mothscale Castle. The forest outside is really dark and gloomy, and the trees wave at me, and I can hear wolves — at least, I'm pretty sure they're wolves — howling all night long. But I like it much better now. If I wasn't here, I wouldn't have found the scroll, and I wouldn't have a True Companion, and I definitely wouldn't have my snow-white steed.

Thoughts of Dora, his big white horse, filled Sam's mind.

She wasn't far away, but if Sam could have had his wish he would have spent the night in the stables.

Aunt Egg, however, had squashed this idea flat. "Only horses live in stables," she had announced. "You, Sam, live in Mothscale Castle. You have a perfectly good bedroom, and I want you IN IT."

Sam had done as he was told. Only Prune ever argued with Aunt Egg. He had gone to bed, but it had been almost impossible to sleep. He had a horse! And Prune had her pony, Weebles! Surely it would be MUCH easier to do the rest of the tasks now, and then he would be a proper knight … He and Prune could ride out together, maybe even into the forest – and who knew what kind of adventures they would—

BANG!

Something hit Sam's
window, making him jump. Ink
spattered over his diary, and only a
wild dive saved the bottle from crashing
to the floor.

BANG!

Sam ran to the window, opened it and
looked out. In the
dimness of the early
morning light, he could
just see Prune waving at
him from the courtyard
far below. When she
saw his head the waving
turned to an imperious
beckoning and Sam gave
her a grin and a thumbs
up. Prune nodded, and
headed for the stables.

"Dandy!" Sam prodded the sleeping doodlebird. "Dandy! Prune's waiting for me!"

The doodlebird sighed. "AWK?"

"OK," Sam agreed. "I'll see you later." And, picking up his shoes, he hurried out of his bedroom.

GOBLINS

Beware – there are goblins living among us!

Within these pages lies a glimpse into their secret world. But read quickly, and speak softly, in case the goblins spot you ...

A riotous, laugh-out-loud funny series from the bestselling author of HUGLESS DOUGLAS, David Melling.

www.hiddengoblins.co.uk